# Admiral of New England

## Captain John Smith and the American Dream

by

John Haden and the Y7 students of King Edward VI Grammar School, Louth

First published by Barny Books
All rights reserved
Copyright © John Haden 2005
No part of this publication may be reproduced or transmitted in any way or by any means, including electronic storage and retrieval, without prior permission of the publisher.

ISBN No:      1.903172.58.6

Publishers:   Barny Books
              Hough on the Hill,
              Grantham,
              Lincolnshire
              NG32 2BB
              Tel: 01400 250246

Printed by:   Allinson Print and Supplies
              Allinson House
              Lincoln Way
              Fairfield Industrial Estate
              Louth LN11 0LS

Copies of this book and the others in the ARIES series, may be obtained from: Julian Bower Associates, Julian Bower House, Louth, Lincolnshire LN11 9QN. Tel: 01507 601254 Please enclose cheque payable to 'Julian Bower Associates' with your order and add £1.00 per copy to cover postage and packing.

# Foreword

In September 1609, a badly burnt soldier was carried from Jamestown Fort, Virginia, to a waiting ship. He was taken down the James River to sail back to England. It seemed that Captain John Smith of Willoughby's leadership of the tiny settlement at Jamestown had come to a sad end.

For the year of his elected Presidency, Smith had led the first permanent English-speaking colony on the shore of North America. He had survived disease and capture by the Algonquin Indians and been spared execution by Powhatan, their great chief, through the pleading of Pocahontas, his eleven year old daughter. Powhatan's people and Smith had traded for food which kept the colony alive through two hard winters.

But Smith's injuries and a new regime at Jamestown ended his contribution to Virginia. He never returned to the colony. His safe arrival in London offered little except pain and disgrace. And yet the second half of John Smith's life, from 1609 to 1631, produced achievements at least as significant as his contribution to Virginia. These years of further exploration, writing and promoting the idea of colonies in America were not so filled with the 'brave adventures' of his youth. But they saw Smith help to establish new settlements to the north of Virginia in the region he was the first to call 'New England'. His vision of how these settlements should operate contributed to the birth of the 'American Dream'.

This short book has been written and illustrated with the help of Y7 students at the King Edward VI Grammar School, Louth, where John Smith completed his formal education in the 1590s. It is the second book in the 'American Roots in English Soil' series, published to celebrate Lincolnshire's rich heritage of Early American history. It is also part of our contribution to the 400th Anniversary of the founding of Jamestown.

## Dreaming of Gold and Spices

The English came to Virginia hoping to find gold, just as the Spanish had done in Mexico and Peru. In their eyes, America was a place of untold riches there for the taking. The poet, John Donne, writing around the time of the first Jamestown voyage, used this picture of America, a continent to be explored as a lover might explore the delights of his beloved:

*Lines from Elegy 19:*
*O my America, my new found land,*
*My kingdom, safeliest when with one man manned*
*My mine of precious stones, my empiry,*
*How blessed am I in this discovering thee!*

Three small ships set out from Blackwall, near London, just before Christmas 1606, carrying 105 men and boys. They were heading for the rivers of the Chesapeake, the great bay north of Raleigh's failed colony at Roanoke and south of the Hudson River, where New York now stands. They were sent by the Virginia Company of London.

Coat of arms of the London Virginia Company

The voyage was a business venture for which the Company had raised money by selling shares to rich individuals and other organisations in the City of London.

The English settled on a swampy island thirty miles from the sea, on the banks of the river they called the James, There they built a military fort, Jamestown. But their dream of finding gold turned to a nightmare as the heat of their first Virginia summer brought sickness and death to this toe-hold on the shores of North America. Amongst them was a young soldier of fortune from Lincolnshire, Captain John Smith. He claimed to have the trappings of a gentleman, with his own coat of arms, but came from a relatively humble background, the son of a tenant farmer. John Smith's early life reflected his motto: 'Vincere est Vivere', 'To Conquer is to Live'.

John Smith's coat of arms, *(from the window in Willoughby church)*

## The American Dream'

In the four hundred years since the first settlement at Jamestown, America has attracted millions of people from Europe seeking a new future. It has become the 'land of the free', where neither your background nor your wealth matter. Even the poorest boy or girl could make it to the top, given ability, ambition and hard work. This is the 'American Dream'.

The English who first landed at Jamestown were subjects of King James I of England. He believed that God had given him the right to be king over all his people. 'Rags-to-riches' stories, like 'Dick Whittington and his Cat', were popular in London at the time but most Englishmen knew their place in the strict pecking order of Tudor and Stuart England. John Smith, the farmer's son, had tried to better himself through service as a soldier but few took him seriously until his toughness and ability to lead men brought him to the top at Jamestown. Many who resented his lack of respect for his social betters, disliked him and tried to get rid of him.

King James I by Molly J.

## *Searching for a way through*

*Another reason for the expedition to Virginia was to find a way through to the Far East, where the English hoped to find valuable spices like nutmeg and pepper and gain from the rich trade in these spices. They thought that the continent of America was very narrow and that there must be a way across Virginia to the Pacific Ocean. Although the search for a Northwest Passage went on for hundreds of years, they could not find a way through. They had to try to establish a settlement which could support itself.*

*The English were not very good at living independently. The Virginian Indians taught them about their food-crops like maize and beans. They also showed the English how to catch the fish which were plentiful in the rivers.*

*Twenty five years before, Drake had sailed round Africa and America to the Far East, but it was a very long way. On such ocean voyages, many sailors suffered from a disease called scurvy. This made them weak, with swollen joints, and they would usually die. Before setting off on the voyage to Virginia or back to England, the ship would load up a large stock of food. When the food was no longer fresh, the sailors would become sick. We now know that fruits like limes, lemons and oranges and fresh fish contain vitamin C so sailors do not suffer from scurvy any more. When Jamestown was founded, they were only beginning to discover this.* *(Kieron S.)*

## Living with the Algonquin

After Jamestown had been established for a year, when most of the other leaders had either died or gone home to England, Captain John Smith became 'President'. He was the youngest of the original council members and the only one who was not a 'gentleman'. He knew that the English depended on the Virginian Indians but he also knew that they would only co-operate if they were sure that the English were strong. By forming a strong link with Powhatan, the Great Chief of the Algonquin people, Smith enabled the settlement to survive. He knew that Powhatan had to be convinved that the English were capable of successfully defending themselves against any attack. Smith always took great care to exchange hostages before any negotiation with the Algonquin, to ensure that they did not double-cross him.

The Algonquin people, who occupied the forests around Jamestown, were part of the great Indian nation of the East Coast of America. They used canoes for fishing and travel on the many rivers of the Chesapeake. Unlike the Plains Indians to the west, they had no horses. They lived in villages of wood-frame houses covered with grass rather than the tepees of the plains. But they shared a pride in their own heritage with all the other American Indian peoples and used the land as a gift to sustain life, rather than a personal possession.

Smith travelled throughout the region, getting to know the different groups of Algonquin, helped by Powhatan and his daughter, Pocahontas. She was only eleven or twelve at the time but she enjoyed visiting Jamestown and saved Smith's life twice. He learnt to speak her language and recorded her peoples' customs, along with the details of their settlements and the rivers of the area. . By trading axes and other goods for food, Smith kept the colony alive through his year of office as President.

Algonquin warrior from John White's collection of paintings.

# Hero or Failure?

Confident and proud, John Smith's statue on Jamestown Island today shows him gazing down the James River towards the sea. It is the image of a hero but the reality in the autumn of 1609 was very different. Smith had been injured in a gunpowder explosion that almost killed him. Powhatan and Pocahontas were told that he had died.

But John Smith survived, just. New leaders had been sent out to the settlement by the Virginia Company and Smith's year of office as President had come to an end. He knew that if he stayed in Jamestown he would be given a very minor role. So in early September, still unable to walk, he got a passage on one of the ships returning to England.

The sailing was delayed while his enemies in Jamestown wrote letters of complaint about him to the leaders of the Virginia Company in London. The letters travelled home with him to the people in London who wanted to believe that Smith had failed.

## The New Charter

Earlier that year, back in London, the Virginia Company had decided to make a fresh start for their Virginia Colony. William Crawshaw preached to the Royal Court, and to the Council of the Virginia Company praising the virtues of Virginia. His theme was that there should be a fresh start with converting the Virginian Indians to Christianity as a higher goal than finding gold or access to the spice trade.

The Virginia Company raised more money by subscription, encouraging rich individuals and companies to buy shares in this new beginning for their Virginia project. They petitioned King James for a new Charter, providing for a single Governor rather than a Council of seven from which a governor was elected annually.

Above all, they recruited more volunteers to go out to Virginia, men and women who would work for the Company for an agreed numbers of years, and then have an opportunity to work for themselves.

The poet, Michael Drayton, wrote an 'Ode to the Virginia Voyage' to encourage as many as could be persauded to sign up for a new voyage:

*You brave heroic minds,*
*Worthy your country's name,*
*That honour still pursue,*
*Go and subdue,*
*Whilst loit'ring hinds*
*Lurk here at home with shame.*

*….And cheerfully at sea*
*Success you still entice*
*To get the pearl and gold*
*And, ours to hold,*
*VIRGINIA,*
*Earth's only paradise!*

The newly appointed Governor and hundreds of new recruits sailed from London in a fleet of ships only to be hit by a hurricane in mid-Atlantic. The Governor, Charter and the other new leaders were separated from the rest and disappeared. The others reached Jamestown in July. With no new Charter or Governor, President Smith insisted on remaining in charge until the early autumn when George Percy, the younger brother of the Earl of Northumberland was elected in his place.

## George Percy as President

It is easy to feel sorry for George Percy. The leadership of the colony was thrust into his hands. He was not a leader. He had little skill in negotiating with the Indians and he had a strong sense of his own importance. He had come to Jamestown in 1607 and survived the early months. It was his journal that recorded the deaths of so many of the English.

When most of the 1609 fleet arrived in the James River with so many new colonists, the colony seemed to be in a stronger state than it had been from the start. Over five hundred English men, and a few English women and children, were living in and around Jamestown. They had three ships, and seven river boats, enough food to last ten weeks and a store well stocked with axes and beads to be traded for food with the Algonquin.

The fort was well defended with twenty four cannons and over one hundred soldiers with plenty of muskets and other weapons. They also had a good stock of livestock, six mares and a stallion, five or six hundred pigs, plenty of chickens and a few goats and sheep. With the colony well established, there was every prospect of a peaceful and successful expansion. But Powhatan now knew that the English were intending to stay in his land. Within a few months of John Smith sailing home, the busy scene at Jamestown turned into a stinking mess sheltering a few survivors.

The Virginia Company's claim for the purpose of the Jamestown settlement, *(from the window in Willoughby church)*

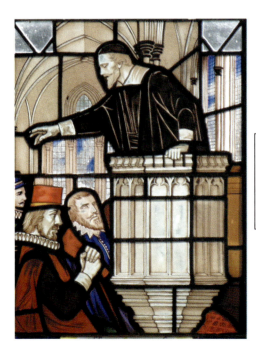

Revd. William Crawshaw's sermon to promote Virginia, *(from the window in Willoughby Church)*

## *The starving time*

Smith's departure literally broke the colony apart. With little effective leadership, life in Jamestown deteriorated rapidly. Smith's friendship with Pocahontas and her father Powhatan had gone and, with it, the trade of corn and other foods between the Algonquin and the English. Powhatan knew that the English could not grow their own crops and although the English wanted the trade to start again, Powhatan was determined to get rid of them.

After ten weeks, the English in Jamestown sent out a group to trade for corn with the Virginian Indians. All of them were killed and when their bodies were found, their mouths were stuffed with corn: the Algonquin were definitely trying to prove a point.

Powhatan destroyed all the English settlers' means of getting food. The English had thought ahead and kept pigs on a separate island called Hog Island. As soon as Powhatan found out, he ordered his men to go to Hog Island and slaughter all the pigs. To stop them catching fish, he had all their boats cut loose.

Powhatan decided to set a trap to attempt to kill the surviving English. He invited them to come out of their fort to trade for corn. Fifty of the English fell into the trap. Most were killed. Only sixteen made it back to Jamestown.

People in Jamestown were starting to get desperate. Those who tried to forage for food usually got caught and murdered by the Algonquin. All the dogs, horses, cats and other animals in the settlement had been eaten, even the rats and mice!

Finally, in the winter of 1609/1610, the English were driven to cannibalism. It was gruesome. Corpses were dug up and butchered to be eaten.

A man called Collins murdered his pregnant wife, slipped his unborn child into the river and ate his wife

*When he was found out, he was hung up by his thumbs until he confessed and then executed.*

*(Bethan H.)*

## Relief arrives

In May 1610, the new leadership which had been sent out from London finally reached the horror that was Jamestown. At first, there seemed to be no-one to welcome them. The houses had been pulled apart by men desparate for firewood and terrified to leave the relative safety of the fort. The new leaders rang the church bell and out of the wreckage of the fort, came walking dead men, crying 'we are starved'. Sixty miserable survivors were left from the five hundred men and women there at the time of John Smith's departure. The leaders re-established the settlement and, once again, Jamestown survived.

## Tribute to Smith's leadership

One of the soldiers who had served under John Smith in Virginia wrote this tribute in appreciation of his leadership of the colony:

*'What shall I say? but thus we lost him, that in all his proceedings made justice his first guide, and experience his second, ever hating baseness, sloth, pride and indignity more than any dangers; that never allowed more for himself than his soldiers with him; ......that loved actions more than words, and hated falsehood and cozenage (cheating) more than death; whose adventures were our lives, and whose loss our deaths.'*

*(One of Smith's men, probably William Fettiplace, from 'The proceedings' 1612).*

## Facing his accusers

But back in London, which John Smith's ship reached in late 1609, the official view of his contribution to the colony was far less rosy. He had made many enemies amongst the gentlemen who had first led the colony and he had quarrelled with the leadership in London of the Virginia Company.

Tactless and openly critical, Smith had scorned their ambition to find gold and a way through to the Pacific. As President, he had concentrated on ensuring the colony's survival by trading for food and exploring the area. He encouraged the settlers to start small scale production of useful things like glass and timber boards. He believed that only those who worked should be fed, no matter what their status was. Of the early leaders, he admired Captain Batholomew Gosnold and the Revd. James Hunt, but Gosnold had died soon after reaching Virginia and Hunt was the Chaplain with little real influence.

The London Company had tried to maintain 'good news' from Virginia from the start by imposing tight censorship over all letters and shipments to and from England. It was an offence to send home unauthorised accounts of the true suffering of the colony and Smith had sent two letters home, setting out the truth as he saw it.

## Smith defends himself

Still recovering from his wounds, Smith prepared to defend himself against the complaints and accusations of those who were offended by the jumped-up farmer's son who had presumed to take over the leadership of Jamestown. He was accused of forcing some of the English to live on oysters, which had in fact saved their lives. The troublesome Dutch in the colony accused him of trying to kill them with rat poison which he completely denied! It was said that he had failed to defend outlying settlements against attack when it had always been his policy to try to co-operate with the Indians and avoid attacks. Worst of all, he was accused of plotting to marry Pocahontas to make himself king, although she was just a child at the time.

The leaders of the Virginia Company wanted to believe that all this was true as there were many in London with a grudge against Smith. Neither he nor they had yet heard of the disaster of the 'starving time' in Virginia.

In Smith's eyes, it was the Council who should be on trial for their failure to send what was actually needed to establish a self-sufficient and stable community. They had attempted to exploit Virginia, to try to make it yield fabulous supplies of gold and jewels, timber and valuable natural products like sassafras. None had been produced in any quantity. They had lost money and were losing the support of the great men of England who had also invested in Virginia. They were looking for someone to blame. With his disdain for privilege and position and his lack of tact, Smith would never be able to defend himself successfully before men who had no personal experience of life in Virginia and no understanding of the need for vigorous leadership.

There is no record of Smith's 'trial' and no record of any conviction or punishment imposed on him. All we know is that the Company's enquiries into what happened in Virginia over the time he was there led to two 'official reports'. The first was brought out in haste in 1610, and claimed that the council had set up the colony 'to preach and baptise into the Christian religion 'poor and miserable souls'. Another purpose was to provide somewhere to dump England's troublesome poor. Lastly, they claimed that Virginia would be a 'fruitful land' providing England with 'necessities…which we are now forced to buy'.

They made no mention of searching for gold or a passage to the Pacific. The report went on to blame the 'errors and discouragements which seem to lie so heavy as almost to press to death this brave and hopeful action'. Fortunately, according to them, the Council of the Company had saved the day by appointing a new governor for the colony and sending out the great fleet in 1609. They then declared that 'no man would acknowledge a superior nor could from this headless and unbridled multitude be anything expected but disorder and riot...'

There was no mention of John Smith's efforts to control the 'unbridled multitude', nor the fact that 'disorder and riot' did not break out until six months after he was wounded and taken home.

## Bad news from Virginia

The whole investigation was overtaken by yet more bad news from Virginia. The ship which had been sent from England with a new charter and new leadership for the colony was reported to be lost. Later in 1610, the news reached London that the Company's appointed leadership had eventually got to Jamestown, but only after the starving time had decimated the colony. In November 1610, the Council put out another 'True Declaration of the estate of the colony in Virginia', hoping to deny 'such scandalous reports as have tended to the disgrace of so worthy an enterprise', and to praise the new governor, Sir Thomas Gates. They even claimed that the man who had eaten his wife had done nothing of the sort but had killed her in a domestic tiff while their larder was full!

By then of course, it was too late. All London knew what had happened but the Council of the Virginia Company went on claiming that the fault lay not with them but with the Colony's lack in the early years of 'an able governor'. Captain John Smith was being written out of the official record.

## Smith strikes back

His response was to publish a record of his own. While living in London and recovering from his injuries, Smith wrote an account of the early years of Jamestown, including a wealth of information about the Algonquin Indians. His exploration of the rivers of the Chesapeake enabled him to draft a map of the whole area and he had the best engraver in the land prepare the plates for printing it.

To make the map more interesting, he agreed with the engraver that copies of pictures of Algonquin Indians and their houses should be included. As none of the soldiers in Smith's expedition had artistic skills, the engraver 'borrowed' images from the pictures which John White had brought back from Raleigh's expedition to Roanoke Island in 1585. Nevertheless, Smith's map of the Chesapeake area continued to be used for over a hundred years and was even used by Virginia and Maryland to help clear up a boundary dispute in 1875!

With this extraordinarily detailed map, John Smith wanted to publish a short book which told the truth about the first two years of Jamestown, but he ran into a problem.

## *Publishing John's Book*

*John Smith had trouble getting his book published. Not enough people liked him in London and they didn't believe what he wrote. Although London was full of printing presses, the Stationers Company had control over all the printers of the City.*

*The Virginia Company could put pressure on the Stationers and stop the printing of Smith's book. When Smith tried to find a printer for his 'A Map of Virginia with a description of the Countreye' which was to be published together with his second book 'The proceedings of the English Colony', two books in one cover, no-one in London would help him.*

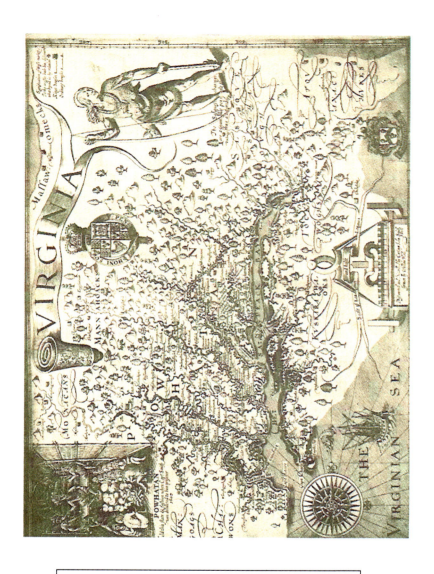

John Smith's Map of Virginia 1612

Outside London at that time, there were only two legal presses in England. These were at the universities of

*Oxford and Cambridge, beyond the control of the London City companies. Because no-one would print his book in London, John Smith must have decided to go to Oxford to get it printed by John Barnes, the University printer. Someone must have helped him, although no-one knows who it was.*

*In the map which went with the book, there is the name Robert Clarke squeezed in which could suggest he was the publisher. However it was done, John's Map and Books were printed.*

*(Chloe B.)*

## Attacking Virginia Company policy

Much of what John Smith wrote was also included in another book, William Strachey's 'History of Travel', also published in 1612.

Here at last were accurate accounts of the early years of Jamestown, written by those who were there. Smith did not mince his words, with an attack on those 'bad natures' …'that will slovenly spit at all things' …'because they found not English cities, nor such fair houses, nor…any of their accustomed dainties, with feather beds and down pillows, taverns and ale-houses in every breathing place, neither such plenty of gold and silver and dissolute liberty as they expected….had little care of anything but to pamper their bellies, to fly away with our pinnaces, or procure their means to return for England. For to them the country was a misery, a ruin, a death, a hell'.

## London contacts

After such strong criticism of those who thought themselves his betters, Smith's chances of ever getting financial support from the Virginia Company of London for further ventures were nil, and he knew it. He stayed in London for a time and must have found a home with one of his friends, as he never owned a house in the city as far as we know. This brought him into contact with a Reverend with an interest in America, Samuel Purchas.

Purchas certainly met Smith some time in 1611 and borrowed from him some of Smith's writing about Virginia. He saw himself as the successor to the great Elizabethan geographer, the Rev Richard Hakluyt, who had published a collection of accounts of all the early voyages to Virginia. Purchas brought Hakluyt's work up to date by gathering together and publishing all that he could find about the Jamestown experience from those who had been there, including the wrtings of John Smith and George Percy.

Purchas' two books were enormous, both in their size and the lengths of their titles. The first edition of his *Purchas His Pigrimage, or Relations of the World and the Religious Observed in All Ages and Places* was published in 1613 and ran to just under a thousand pages. Included are long passages of Smith's own work from *Map of Virginia*. The learned Reverend put into print in London what the Virginia Company managed to stop under Smith's own name!

Purchas' second work had an even longer and more ridiculous title: *Hakluytus Posthumus, or Purchas His Pilgrimes, containing a History of the World in Sea Voyages and Land Travels by Englishmen and Others etc.* It had over four thousand pages when it was published in 1625. The two are often referred to as *Pilgrimage* and *Pilgrimes*, which is all very confusing! But they were a publishing success in a London eager for the truth about Virginia.

Rev Samuel Purchas (*from the window in Willoughby Church*)

## London's stinking streets

Purchas and Smith lived in the busy, filthy City of London, a place which disease made almost as dangerous as Jamestown. The houses were crammed into narrow streets into which everyone tipped their rubbish and their sewage. Dogs scavenged the gutters and rats ran through the rubbish, spreading disease and fleas. Herds of cattle on their way to slaughter added to the muck under foot and the horses of the richer people made their contribution to the stench.

London street from a wood cut of the period.

## *Dysentery, plague, smallpox and typhoid, disease in London and America*

Four of the worst diseases which killed thousands of people in London were dysentery, plague, typhoid fever and smallpox. The plague was spread by fleas which lived on rats in the gutters and drains of the overcrowded streets. They sucked blood from infected rats and passed the disease on to people by biting through their skin. After two to six days, the plague symptoms started: headaches, weakness, fever, aching limbs and delirium. The lymph nodes would swell and be very painful, forming 'bubees' which might burst releasing pus. This form of plague was called bubonic, and sometimes black patches formed on the skin, hence the old term for the disease, the 'black death'. This disease was bad enough, but even more serious was the pneumonic form when the lungs were infected. Death would be almost certain.

There was a major outbreak of the plague in 1603, when over 200,000 Londoners died and the coronation ceremony for James I had to be postponed.

---

There was at the time a fashion for love poetry on the theme of the flea, as the insect had liberty to hop from the lover to the beloved! John Donne wrote these lines:

*Mark but this flea, and mark in this,*
*How little that thou deny'st me is;*
*Me it sucked first, and now sucks thee,*
*And in this flea, our two bloods mingled be;*
*Confess it, this cannot be said*
*A sin, or shame, or loss of maidenhead,*
*Yet this enjoys before it woo,*
*And pampered swells with one blood made of two,*
*And this alas is more than we would do.*

Small pox was another very infectious disease, spread by a virus which has now been eliminated world wide. In the 17th century, it was very common in London, and spread quickly amongst people living close together. The English and other Europeans took smallpox to America where it wiped out whole populations of Native Americans who had no natural resistance.

After about two week from being infected, the person suffered from a high fever, aches in the head and body and vomiting. Red spots appeared which changed to watery craters on the skin, drying out to leave horrible scabby scars. Some did recover, with permanent disfigurement, but thousands died.

Typhoid and dysentery were both carried by bacteria in water or food, which infected the digestive system. Typhoid fever caused a red rash on the abdomen and chest, headaches and nosebleeds. The patient's temperature rose in a characteristic stepladder fashion, and in serious cases, the massive infection spread throughout the gut. This was usually fatal. The disease can now be controlled by high standards of personal hygiene and clean water supplies, but neither were common in the 17th century. James I had a horror of water and, if he washed at all, he would only wash his fingers! The last major outbreak of typhoid in this region was in Lincoln in 1905 when 118 people died and clean water had to be brought in from Newark.

Dysentery is an infection and ulceration of the lower part of the bowel which causes severe diarrhoea and the passing of mucus and blood, hence its old name, 'the bloody flux'. It can now be treated easily with drugs, but there was no cure in 1600. You either recovered or died, and it was particularly dangerous for children

*(Sophie T.)*

## Travelling in London

Those who wanted to avoid walking through the stinking streets of London could travel by river. Down river or 'eastward ho' for the boatmen, the Tower of London marked the end of the City. Across the many arched London Bridge, where buildings almost blocked the road, Southwark offered brothels and bear-pits and theatres free from the limitations of the city authorities. This was the London of Shakespeare and Marlow, and the flourishing playhouses of the early Stuart years.

From the end of London Bridge, the road led south through Kent to Dover and the rest of the world. The separate city of Westminster, with the royal palace of Whitehall, was upstream, or 'west-ward ho' from London Bridge. The old gothic Cathedral of St Paul's dominated the sky-line much as Lincoln Minster still dominates that city today.

The City Companies, the Mercers and the Grocers, the Fishmongers and the Cordwainers and over forty others, controlled all the trade of the City. Each had a livery Hall and organised the workforce of a particular trade into apprentices, company men and freemen of the city until they rose to the status of liverymen of the Company. In theory at least, a poor apprentice could rise through the ranks to be Lord Mayor of London. This is what happened to the real Richard Whittington in the 14th century. He walked to London from the country and became an apprentice, rising through the ranks to be Lord Mayor three times.

The story of Dick Whittington and his cat makes a good pantomime. It was first performed as a play in 1605 and has entertained families ever since. The bells of London rang out just as he was about to give up and go home. He thought they sang 'turn again Whittington, Lord Mayor of London', so he went back and made his fortune. John Smith did not hear any bells but he too had to think how to start again.

Most of the Company Halls were lost when the Great Fire swept through London in 1666. Lost too were the narrow streets of half-timbered houses and most of the parish churches. The London of the early seventeenth century would have looked much more like the streets of York, where the Tudor and earlier buildings have survived.

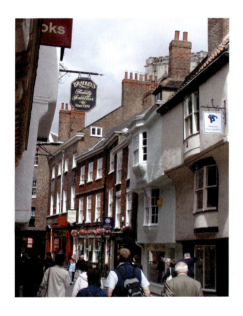

Narrow streets in York today, much like the houses in Stuart London

The London skyline in 1616, by Jenny V., after Jan Visscher.

## Trying again, in Jamestown and in London

The new regime in Jamestown did eventually succeed in making the settlers behave sensibly. New laws were introduced which improved life in the colony for all, reducing the contamination of the well on which they all depended. Those who were caught doing 'the necessities of nature' near to the fort were punished by whipping. The numbers dying from drinking bad water and catching diseases began to fall.

In London, King James decided to do something about the water supply. Although the Romans had brought the idea of aquaducts to Britain, few in London in the early 17th century had clean drinking water. Water for the city was lifted from the River Thames by a great waterwheel on London Bridge, which also had one of the largest public latrines in the City.

Londoners also had water from shallow wells in their gardens.. Both sources could be very contaminated as the sewage from the streets and alleys found its way into the water. Men, women and even children drank beer as the brewing process killed most of the bacteria in the water.
King James authorised the Corporation of London to begin a great scheme to bring fresh water into the city.

The south end of London Bridge with the heads of traitors on pikes

## *The story of the New River*

The New River started construction in 1609. It was designed to bring clean water from a long way north of the city by a canal to a pool in what is now Islington. The course had first to be very accurately surveyed so that it followed the 100 ft contour. During the building of it, overseen by Hugh Middleton, the banks had to be strengthened with clay and 157 bridges built where roads cross the course. At one point, the River went through the royal estates, at Theobalds Park, but, luckily for Middleton, James I was interested in the project and let him carry on free of charge. The New River came to a standstill near Wormley in 1610 due to landowners refusing to sell their land but the project was eventually finished in 1613. You can find parts of the New River marked on maps of London today as it still brings water nearer to the City.

*(Dominic B.)*

## Death of Prince Henry 1612

But the New River was not finished in time to save King James' oldest son, Prince Henry. He was a strong supporter of the Virginia venture and very interested in the Navy. Sir Walter Raleigh wrote a series of pieces all addressed to the Prince including his 'Observations and notes concerning the Royal Navy'. In this Raleigh wrote that a man of war should be strongly built, swift, stout-sided, able to carry her guns in all weathers and not burdened with too many heavy guns. Henry encouraged the Navy to build such ships which were needed to defend England's growing trade interest in the Far East and across the Atlantic. Henry did not get on well with his father. James had imprisoned Raleigh in the Tower and Henry is said to have commented 'none but my father would keep such a bird in a cage'.

In October 1612, when Henry was only nineteen, he caught typhoid fever from contaminated Thames water and on November 6th, he died. Ironically, the portrait of the Prince with a red face and wearing red leggings mimicked the symptom of that disease, in which the infection causes a bright red rash all over the body.

Henry, Prince of Wales, by Holly B. from the portrait by Robert Peake the Elder

With Henry dead, the succession passed to Charles, his younger brother. He was a shy and stuttering young man who had none of the energy or enthusiasm for England's colonies of his brother. After the long dispute between Charles and Parliament ended in the Civil War, Charles was tried and beheaded in 1649.

## Marmaduke invests part of his fortune.

By 1614, the City Companies were losing interest in investing further in Virginia, but there were still rich men in London who could be tempted. A clothworker called Rawdon had the good fortune, literally, of marrying a very rich heiress. He wanted to make even more money. With three other London 'adventurers', Rawdon planned to send a 'fleet' of just two ships to the northen part of Virginia, partly in search of gold and copper but also to make money from fishing and whaling. The Dutch had already made a lot of money from the rich fishing in that area and there were said to be many whales who would yield valuable whale oil.

Rawdon recruited John Smith to lead this voyage and the two ships set off from England. They took with them a young Patuxet man from the Cape Cod area called Squanto as a guide.

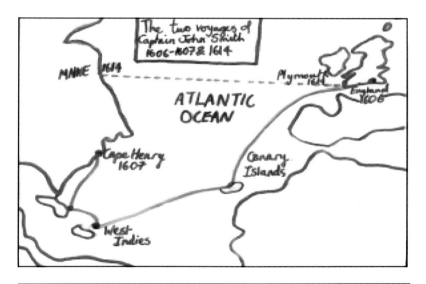

Sketch map of Smith's two voyages across the Atlantic by Jenni V.

John Smith chose the northern route which had been pioneered by Bartholomew Gosnold, due west across the Atlantic.

They reached Monhegan Island off the coast of Maine towards the end of April after navigating across the ocean.

## 17th Century Navigation

*At that time, sailors used an astrolabe to work out the ship's latitude by holding it up to the sun at noon. They worked out the ship's north-south position from the angle of the sun, using a set of tables to do the calculation.*

*For direction, they used a compass with the needle attached to a flat disc so that the whole thing always pointed north and each $11^{1/4}°$ mark had a name, such as North, North-west, North-north-west etc.*

Nautical compass by Abigail M.

*To work out how fast they were going, a log-line with a series of knots and a board at the end was thrown into the sea just as a one-minute timer like a sand-glass egg timer was started. By counting the number of knots that ran out in a minute, the sailor would know the speed. We still use the term 'knots' for speeds at sea today*

*It was difficult to work out the ship's longitude (how far east-west they had gone) because chronometers which measure time accurately had not been invented.*

*The maps of America that were available at the time were pretty useless to John Smith. When they knew they were near to the American coast, they would have used a sounding lead to measure how deep the water was so that the ship did not hit the shore!*

*(Dominic B.)*

## Whaling and fishing

Monhegan Island is a rocky outcrop off what is now the coast of Maine. It may seem difficult to find, but there were many English, French and Dutch fishing boats heading in that direction as the island offered a good anchorage.

After Smith's two ships reached the island, they started to hunt for whales. This proved fruitless as the whales were very large, very fast and very fierce! We now think that they were probably Rouqual or Finback whales. As Smith reported, 'they could not kill any… being a kind of Jubartes and not the whale that yields …oil as we expected'. There would be no rich reward from whale oil.

Failing to catch a whale (!) by Molly J.

Smith decided to fall back on fishing. He knew that dried cod, called stock fish or 'Poor John', fetched a good price in the countries of Southern Europe. Catholics there were dependant on dried fish to fulfil the Church requirement that everyone should eat fish on Fridays. Fresh fish taken inland on a donkey did not stay edible for long in the summer heat and there were an awful lot of Catholics in inland Spain, Portugal and Italy!

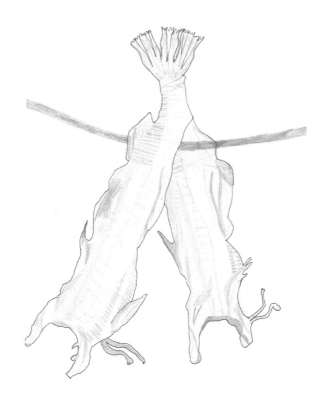

Stockfish drying in the wind by Jenni V. This form of dried cod is still used in many recipes in Portugal to make their national dish *bacalhao*

Smith left a party of men on Monhegan Island with Captain Hunt to fish for cod and set off in a small ship with just eight men along the coast of what was then called 'Northern Virginia'. He knew that the French had already made money from trapping animals like beaver and foxes and selling the furs, and decided to combine this with his exploration of the region.

## Fishing

*In about a month, the fifteen men left on Monhegan Island caught 60,000 cod. They filleted and dried them by hanging them on lines.*

(Sean P.)

John Smith sailed west along the coast of what is now Maine. He surveyed the area, 'from point to point, isle to isle, harbor to harbor' in his shallop or small ship and landed on the shore to trap for furs whenever they could. He found that the Virginian Indians of these northern areas spoke a language very similar to the Algonquin of the Jamestown area. This enabled him to make contact with the people and record the Indian names of settlements on the coast and up the rivers. He also noted their names for all the capes and bays as he went and recorded the features of each part of the coast.

Mapping the coast from a small boat or shallop, by Caitlin P.

It was a meticulous piece of map-making and at each place, Smith noted what the coast was like. In the north, what is now Maine, he described what he saw as a country 'rather to afright than delight' with 'craggy rocks and rocky isles' but with extraordinary stocks of fish.

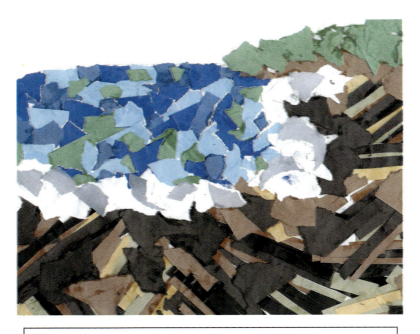

Collage of the coast of Maine by Kate F. and Alice S.

As Smith's small ship sailed on west and south along the coast, the shore became less rocky and barren until he reached what is now the north of Massachusetts, and the more gentle rivers and beaches of the Agawam/Ipswich area. He described this area as 'the paradise of those parts' and the people as 'very kind but, in their fury, very valiant'. It seems that when the English landed, they got a warm reception of arrows but were friends by the time they left.

Crane beach, Massachusetts, by Elyse T.

Further south, the coast was gentler, with sandy beaches and fertile countryside. Beyond Massachusetts Bay, Smith sailed into another bay, with an Indian village called Accomack. '..an excellent harbour, good land: and no want of anything but industrious people. After much kindness, upon a small occasion over nothing, we fought – also with forty or fifty of those. Though some were hurt and some slain, yet within an hour after, they became friends.'

This bay of Accomack, and the next village of Patuxet, were to become the base for just such a group of 'industrious people' about six years later. They were called the Pilgrim Fathers and their settlement, Plymouth. Smith sailed on into Cape Cod Bay, in the wake of Bartholemew Gosnold's 1602 voyage and out to the point of Cape Cod. One of Gosnold's sailors had described the Cape in glowing terms as having 'fat and lustie' soil, with an 'abundance of strawberries', 'great store of deer', and 'fowles in great plenty' (Cape Cod: John Brereton. 1602)

John Smith was much less impressed, describing the Cape as 'onely a headland of high hills of sand, overgrowne with shrubbie pines, hurts and such trash' (John Smith 1614) but the Cape sheltered an excellent harbour. They left Squanto among his own people, sailed on around the Cape and down the Atlantic shore. At the swamps around what is now Eastham, they decided to go no further and turned back north again. Smith and all his men returned to Monhegan Island with all his survey records and a small cargo of furs. He left Captain Hunt and his men on the island to complete the drying of more fish before taking it directly to the markets of Spain. Smith's ship set sail for England with the beaver, martin and otter skins.

Hunt took his ship down to the Massachusetts coast, reaching the Cape Cod area. There, Hunt and his men landed and captured a group of Patuxet and Nauset Indians, taking them on board his ship and sailing off to Spain. Amongst them was the unfortunate Squanto.

## *Squanto - the boy who traded his freedom for a cup of peas- by a child of the Pilgrim Fathers*

*This is the story told to me when I was a young boy and our colony was new. A Native American called Squanto told it to me and it is the story of his life. A long time ago, before the Pilgrim Fathers arrived to build Plymouth Plantation, Squanto lived where Plymouth stands today, in the village of the Patuxet people.*

*'I was walking along the shore with some of my friends when we saw the sails of a ship on the horizon. We watched it come closer and closer. The sailors on board saw us and threw us what I later found out was a cup of peas and some bread which we picked up and ran to the shore to eat it.*

*I loved the taste of the peas, so when we had finished, I ran back across the golden sand with the cup in my hand to the ship. I ran up the gangway and slowly walked across the hot, sticky deck and gave back the cup.*

*They treated my friends and me kindly so when they left I went with them.*

*It was 1605 and I arrived in England with Captain George Weymouth (the captain of the ship). He took me and a few other boys we had picked up in America to a man called Sir Ferdinando Gorges in England where we learned English and lived as servants in his house. Then in 1614 Captain John Smith took me with him to America. When he had finished his mapping of the coast, he planned to leave me at my home. But Captain Thomas Hunt had other ideas. He took me as a guide to my home area and captured more men of my people rather than letting me go home.*

*He then sailed us back across the Atlantic to Malaga in Spain where he sold us into slavery, but I was bought by some friendly Christian monks for £20. They nursed me back to health from the weak and ill self I had become during the journey to Spain and inside the slaves' quarters. They tried to convert me to Christianity. Eventually, I found a ship sailing to Newfoundland, where one of Gorges' old captains found me, a man called Thomas Dermer. He recognised me as 'Sir Ferdinando's Indian' and decided to take me back yet again to England where Gorges gave us another mission on the New England coast. That was how I came to return to the area of my own people. But it was a sad homecoming. While I had been away, the smallpox sickness had come and all the Patuxet had died.*

*In November 1620 the English landed in the Mayflower at the place where my village used to be and started to build Plymouth I walked down the street and greeted them in perfect English. You should have seen the look on their faces! Over the next few years I helped them settle in, trade and grow their own crops. And that, children, is the story of my life.'*

*In 1622, Squanto, our Native American friend, was ill with Indian fever. As he lay dying he asked our governor,*

William Bradford to pray for him so *"he could go to the white man's heaven"*. He gave all his possessions to our community. Our Governor said that he was a *'special instrument sent of God for our good'*.

*(Kyle F.)*

## Planning a new Colony

When Smith got back to England, his cargo of furs and fish was sold. He started to think about a new plan to establish colonies, not in the southern area of Virginia, but just to the north of Cape Cod, in the area for which the Plymouth Virginia Company had the settlement rights.

The area of 'Virginia' under the 'control' of the Plymouth Virginia Company, between 38° and 45° N. This overlapped the London Company's area between 34° and 41° N.

# Exploring the world and the heavens

While John Smith was exploring Virginia, the Frenchman Samuel de Champlain was exploring what is now Canada. In 1608, he founded the city of Quebec. In 1609, the Englishman Henry Hudson discovered the straits far north of Newfoundland, which bear his name and lead to the great Hudson's Bay. The London East India Company began to open up trade routes to the East around the foot of Africa, to India, Java and Siam.

As these men explored the earth, others explored the heavens with newly invented instruments like the telescope. **Galileo Galilei** built his own and used it to look at the planet Jupiter. He found that it had its own moons, just like the earth. He recorded in his notebook in June 1610 what he saw on a series of nights and realised that these moons were in orbit around the planet. One night, he saw two spots of light on one side of the planet and none on the other. On the next there were three, one to the right of the planet and on the next, four, with three on the right. On the fourth night, he saw four spots, all to the right.

Galileo realised that these spots of light were moons moving in orbits around the planet, sometimes visible from earth and sometimes in front of or behind Jupiter. From these observations, Galileo worked out a whole new theory of planetary motion and suggested that the earth must travel around the sun.

This idea was so shocking at the time that it got Galileo into trouble with the church authorities. They taught that the earth kept still while the sun moved across the heavens and forced him to publicly deny his own theory. He had to agree that the earth was the static centre of the universe, but he is said to have muttered under his breath 'and yet it moves'.

Galileo's notes of his telescope observations as he recorded them on four consecutive nights in June 1610

Galileo Galilei by Abigail M.

# *Exploring the Human Body - William Harvey*

William Harvey was an English doctor in the 17th century. As doctor to King Charles I, he earned a considerable amount for this. He has also given us some of our most important information about the human body. He put into practise the scientific principle, "Don't think, experiment." While John Smith was exploring America, Galileo was exploring the night sky and Harvey was exploring the human body.

Harvey was fascinated by the way blood flowed through the human body. He knew that blood was not propelled through the body by a pulsing action in the arteries, which is what most people believed at the time. After carefully dissecting and observing humans and animals, he decided that the heart pumped the blood in a circular course through the body.

His work was supported by the King, which helped Harvey to make another discovery. He was the first to point out that all mammals reproduce by an egg being fertilised by a sperm. (Text: Charlotte O.; Portrait: Kate F.)

## Seeking support in the West Country

John Smith still wanted to establish a new colony in the northern area of Virginia. He tried to persuade backers in both London and Plymouth in the West Country to support him. Having fallen out with the London Virginia Company, he knew that he would not get support from the London City Companies, but hoped that rich merchants there might be persuaded, as Marmaduke Reardon had been. At first he thought that he had a promise of the use of four ships and enough London money to take a party of settlers to America. The promised ships never materialised and John Smith left London with a paltry £200.

He had more success in Plymouth. The Plymouth or Second Virginia Company was established under the same 1606 Charter as the First or London Company. Both were given authority to settle the coast of America between the Spanish in Florida and the French in Nova Francia. Smith met with the Plymouth merchants and leaders hoping that they would back him as they had tried to make a settlement in the area almost ten years before.

## New Colony in the North.

In the same year that Jamestown was founded, the Plymouth company had sent two ships, the 'Mary and John' and the 'Gift of God' across the Atlantic. They sailed with 120 settlers to the northern coast of 'their' region. They reached Monhegan Island by the direct route and then sailed south-west to the estuary where the Sagadahoc River runs into the sea. There they built a fort, houses, a stockade and a storehouse, planning to set up a permanent settlement. It became known as the Sagadahoc colony.

The English at Sagahadoc established an alliance with the local Indians. Still hoping to find a route through to the Pacific, they asked the local Indians about a 'great sea to the west'. The obliging Indians told them that they knew of such a sea, which was 'only seven days march inland'. Their leader, George Popham, wrote excitedly to King James to tell him the good news of this route to 'the southern ocean, reaching to the regions of China, which unquestionably cannot be far from these parts'. But the helpful and truthful Indians must have been referring to the great inland Lake Ontario, which was only about 28 miles to the west of where they were.

Winter came early this far north and the colony ran short of food. With the coming of the spring, supply ships brought them enough for the summer. Although they could have stayed, they decided to return to England, rather than face another freezing winter.

After this discouraging start, the Plymouth Company's interest in a northern colony stalled until the military governor of Plymouth, Sir Ferdinando Gorges, took up the challenge. He had been been involved in all the early Plymouth interest in North America and was convinced that if London could establish an American colony, so could Plymouth.

Dr Matthew Sutcliffe, Dean of Exeter Cathedral, (*from the window in Willoughby Church)*

The one thing they lacked was the money to back the project. Smith's £200 from London would not get them far. He travelled all over Devon to try to raise money but without much success, although he did persuade the wealthy Dean of Exeter, Dr Matthew Sutcliffe, to invest. Eventually, there was enough to prepare for a voyage.

## 'New England' to rival 'Nouvelle France'

The French had called the region to the north of the Popham colony, 'Nouvelle-France'. It was John Smith who hit on the idea of calling the area between the French territory in the north and Cape Cod in the south, 'New England'. The merchants and sailors of Plymouth were interested in the profits to be made from fishing and furs, but Gorges wanted a colony.

Under his leadership, the Plymouth Company appointed John Smith to 'manage their authority in those parts', a task which he readily accepted. With his new role, they granted him a new title of 'Admiral of New England'. Although there was neither fleet to command nor territory to administer, the Plymouth merchants were impressed by Smith's plans and agreed to provide him with four ships for a great voyage to 'New England'

They planned to follow the pattern of the 1614 voyage, with the majority focusing on fishing and whale-oil, and any other valuable cargo they could find. Smith and a small group of settlers would find a good place for a colony and sit out the winter until a new supply ship could reach them in 1616. Thomas Dermer was to be second in command with three other gentlemen leading a small group of soldiers. Six men went who were to 'learn to be sailors'!

## Off to America, again

In March 1615, John Smith was once more on board ship bound for America leading his two ship 'fleet'. They did not get far. A violent storm hit them less than two hundred miles out from Plymouth. One ship was lost and Smith's ship proved to be unseaworthy. She lost all three of her masts with almost all her sails. They had no choice but to limp back to England with only a small sprit-sail flapping in the wind.

Off to America acoss the vast and furious ocean by Elyse T

When they got back to Plymouth, undaunted by this experience, Smith persuaded Gorges to find them another, much smaller, ship and they set sail again in late June 1615. This time it was not the weather but another hazard of sea travel that frustrated them.

## *Pirates*

*In October 1615, somewhere in the Atlantic Ocean, an English pirate named Fry sighted Captain John Smith's small, lonely ship and gave chase. The pirates pursued them for two days. Their ship was more than twice the size of Smith's ship and they had thirty six guns to John's four. There were eighty pirates but only fourteen crew members for Smith. Half of the pirates' crew were also 'master gunners'.*

*The only advantage for Smith was the raging sea which made it almost impossible for them to board Smith's ship. Even though Smith had so many disadvantages, he still wanted to fight! The frightened crew didn't, so they tried to bribe the pirates to leave them alone by offering them gold. Somehow, the pirates managed to get across to Smith's ship although he refused to come out of his cabin to meet them.*

*The pirates found nothing of value on Smith's ship and inquired their destination and purpose. This revealed that Smith was the Captain. Some of the pirates miraculously recognised Smith as they had served under him before. They would have joined him if he had captained them again. He refused to be a pirate captain so the pirates went back to their ship and sailed away!*

*(Luke T.)*

## Attacked by the French

Smith sailed on towards America, on a course due west into the setting sun. When night fell and the wind was light, it must have been very peaceful after all the excitement of storms and pirate attack.

Sailing west at night by Holly B.

Their luck did not last. Two French pirate ships spotted them near to the islands of the Azores. Although England and France were not at war, the French commanded them to surrender. Smith's reaction was to threaten to blow up his ship, and although shots were fired at them, they got away. Four days later, however, four French warships overtook them. Smith's officers begged him to surrender, and having discovered that the French were Protestant ships from La Rochelle, Smith allowed them to board his ship on the understanding that they would be treated fairly.

The French sailors took what they wanted from the English ship and most of the crew were transferred to the French ships. When a wind blew up, the remaining English sailors saw their chance to escape and sailed off without John Smith who was still on board one of the French vessels, alone with nothing but 'his cap, breeches, and waistcoat'!

For the next few months he was an unwilling witness to the attacks by the French ships on shipping of many nations. When they were attacking English, Scottish, and Dutch ships, Smith was kept as a prisoner in the French ship's gun-room but when they attacked a Spanish man-o-war carrying treasure back from the West Indies, Smith joined in the fighting and thus could claim a share of the prize.

Near to the French coast at La Rochelle, he had a chance to escape. In the midst of a storm, he stole one of the ship's boats, and slipped away in the darkness and confusion. Using an infantry half-pike as a paddle and a bucket as a bailer, he tried for twelve hours to get to the shore somewhere near the Isle de Ré. Exhausted and cold, he was carried by the wind and tide down into the mouth of the River Garonne where men hunting waterfowl found him on the mud, 'near drowned and half dead, with water, cold and hunger'.

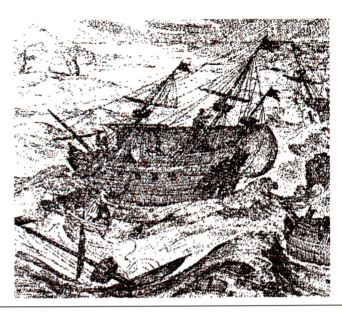

Smith escaping from the French ship at the height of the storm

When he had recovered, John Smith went to the port of La Rochelle and made a formal complaint to the French Naval Authorities. He had been treated badly and piracy was after all a crime. Never one to stay quiet, Smith also complained to the English ambassador in Bordeaux and asked for his share of the value of the Spanish treasure-ship. Although this had been captured by piracy, it had come ashore in the storm. It was therefore a wreck, which Smith could claim against. The law was on his side. He left Bordeaux confident that he would be paid.

By the time he got back to Plymouth, the promised share seems to have been forgotten but he did manage to track down his mutinous crew who had abandoned him to the French in mid-Atlantic. According to his own account, he 'laid them by the heels', whatever that means!

Returning from Plymouth to London, he began the task of setting out the details of his one and only New England voyage for all to read, completing his 'Description of New England or Observations and Discoveries in North America' in time for publication in June 1616.

With the book, Smith published an accurate map of the whole area, decorated with a fine engraving of himself by the young Dutch artist, Simon van de Passe. This is the only likeness of John Smith drawn during his lifetime.

Simon van de Passe's portrait of Captain John Smith, drawn from life, which has been used as the model for his likeness by sculptors and artists ever since.

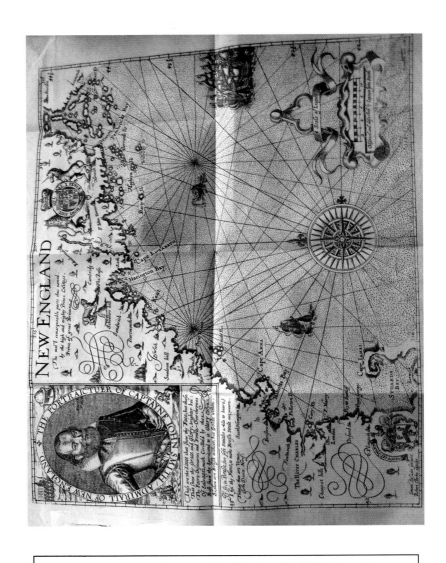

John Smith's 'Map of New England' printed in 1616, from the surveying he completed in 1614.

## John Smith's Map of New England

John Smith's Map of New England, (the northern part of Virginia), was based on his exploration of the area in 1614. Having had such problems publishing his Virginia map in London, he wanted to make it as important as possible, so he wrote to Charles, Prince of Wales, inviting him to chose new names for features on the map

The Native American settlements on the map already had names which John Smith had recorded himself. Smith had to list both the original and Charles' names in his book, which accompanied the map. As there were so many changes, this was extremely difficult. But once someone important was involved, a lot more people would be interested and impressed, and buy the map.. This brought John Smith money which he desperately needed

*Some of these names given by Charles have stuck and are still in use today. For example, the Charles River, which the Prince named after himself. However some have been changed. Smith had to include two lists of names in the book which was published with the map, which must have been very confusing!*

| The old names. | The new names. |
|---|---|
| Cape *Cod*. | Cape *Iames*. |
| The Harbor at Cape *Cod*. | *Milforth* hauen. |
| *Chawum*. | *Barwick*. |
| *Accomack*. | *Plimoth*. |
| *Sagoquas*. | *Oxford*. |
| *Massachusets* Mount. | *Cheui[o]t* hills. |
| *Massachusits* Riuer. | *Charles* Riuer. |
| *Totan*. | *Fa[l]mouth*. |
| A great Bay by Cape *Anne*. | *Bristow*. |
| Cape *Tragabigsanda*. | Cape *Anne*. |

*Captain Bartholomew Gosnold had named Cape Cod, while Prince Charles decided to change it to Cape James. This name was never used and it has always been called Cape Cod*

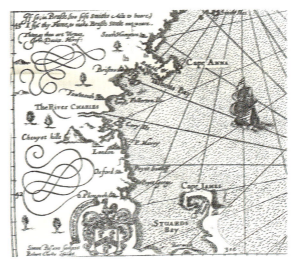

*Most of the names came from England, like Plymouth, Cambridge and Sandwich. When the Pilgrim Fathers came to Plymouth, they had seen it on John Smith's map and kept the name.*

*(Charlotte O.)*

## Leopard, Cougar or Jaguar

One of the mysteries of this map is the animal which decorates inland New England. It looks like a leopard, complete with spots and a long tail, but there are no leopards in North America and as far as we know there never have been. There are still large cats called Cougars, Pumas, Mountain Lions or Panthers, but those in North America are grey or red-brown in colour and only the kittens have spots.

From the south of the USA right down to north Argentina, bigger cats called jaguars are still found in woodland and wilderness areas. They are almost as big as a full grown African Leopard, and have similar coats, with rosette-like spots.

The big black cat from John Smith's Map of New England by Alice S.

Some are almost black in colour. Could the animal in John Smith's map be a jaguar, or is it a leopard which the artist imagined lived in America? People in London would certainly have seen leopards as they were sometimes kept by the very rich as part of a menagerie (zoo). But had they ever seen a jaguar?

## Pocahontas in London

While Smith was busy with his map and book, a visitor from America arrived in London.

## *Meeting Pocahontas again*

*Pocahontas was a Native American woman, the daughter of the most powerful leader in North East America. John Smith and Pocahontas had become friends as Pocahontas had saved Smith's life on two occasions. In 1616, Pocahontas came to London with her husband, John Rolfe, and her baby son, Thomas. Her English name was Lady Rebecca Rolfe. When John Smith learned about Pocahontas' visit, he wrote a long letter to Queen Anne (wife of King James I) asking her to treat Pocahontas like a 'Princess', as technically she was. The queen agreed and when Pocahontas arrived with her family, she was treated with a great deal of respect.*

*Smith did not visit Rebecca Rolfe until late in 1616. When she first saw John Smith, she turned away. Pocahontas would have probably been angry and upset that Smith had not visited her in her eight months in England. In 1617, the Rolfe family decided to return to Virginia. Unfortunately, on the journey down the river Thames, she fell ill, possibly with tuberculosis. Within a few days, she was dead. The Indian Princess' death was followed a year later by the death of her father, Powhatan.*

*(Bethan H.)*

# Three portraits by Kate F.

Pocahontas as a girl, when she saved John Smith's life in Virginia.

Queen Anne, to whom John Smith wrote about Pocahontas.

Pocahontas just before she died at Gravesend, probably of TB.

## Death of Sir Walter Raleigh

Raleigh was still in the Tower, having been convicted of treason after a plot against the King. Many think that he was innocent but James disliked him, partly because he had been such a favourite of Queen Elizabeth. Raleigh had backed the failed colony at Roanoke and was still keen to have a colony of his own.

When he was 62 in 1617, King James released him from the Tower, although still under sentence of death, to plan and lead an expedition to Guyana in South America which was said to have reserves of gold. The King insisted that Raleigh should do nothing to offend the Spanish as the war with Spain was over and there was a plan for his son Charles to marry a Spanish Princess.

It all went wrong. Raleigh got into a fight with the Spanish. He knew that he was doomed but sailed all the way back to England to face execution as a traitor. He was taken out to Tower Green in October 1618. Before he was beheaded with an axe, he felt the blade and said, 'This is sharp medicine, but a sure cure for all diseases and miseries'.

## Links with the Pilgrim Fathers

Plymouth plantation, the American home of the Pilgrim Fathers by Molly J.

For another year or two, John Smith remained in London, but on the other side of the North Sea, in the Dutch city of Leyden, a group of very religious Englishmen were planning for the future of their families. Smith called them 'Brownists', the term which good members of the Church of England used to describe those who wished to 'separate' from the King's Church.

They had escaped from England in 1608 after King James had insisted on all Ministers obeying Church Law and outlawing Separatist congregations. They were also called the Scrooby Separatists because many of them came from the villages around Scrooby in north Nottinghamshire, near to the Lincolnshire town of Gainsborough.

These very religious people had settled in the more tolerant Protestant land of Holland where John Smith had himself fought against the Spanish as a teenager. The English Separatist families lived for a time in the Dutch city of Leyden but then planned to move again to find a new home in America. They sent men to England to see whether the Virginia Company would let them settle in Virginia and also looked at the possibility of going to Guyana in South America or to New England. Eventually they got permission to move to Virginia on the understanding that they would not trouble the King's Church in the colony.

John Smith was in touch with their leaders and offered to act as their guide and military expert as he knew both Virginia and New England but they decided that his help would be too expensive. Instead, they bought his books and maps. They sailed in the Mayflower and in March 1620, arrived off Cape Cod having intended to settle much further south.

They believed that God led them to the American shore in the Cape Cod area. Some of them wanted to sail south again to get to the area where they had planned to settle. When they set off, a fierce storm convinced them that they should stay in the bay sheltered by Cape Cod. There they established their new life, in the place that they knew was called Plymouth. That was its name on John Smith's map.

In his writings, Smith commented: 'ignorance caused them, for more than a year, to endure a wonderful deal of misery with an infinite patience; saying My Books and Maps were much better cheap to teach them than myself ...For want of good take-head (advice) ..forty of them died and threescore were left in most miserable estate at New Plymouth where their ship left them'.

## Writing in London

John Smith was now to prove the truth of the old saying 'the pen is mightier than the sword'. He had been President of Virginia for a year. He had published three books and two maps, describing his exploration of much of the coast of North East America. Above all, he had survived in a world where most men would have died, from war, disease, or exhaustion!

He first published new editions of his book on New England, adding the word 'Trials' because he included the first few difficult years of the Plymouth Colony, and the great Indian attack on the Virginia colony.

Jamestown had become the centre of a new business venture. John Rolfe had brought new varieties of tobacco seed to Virginia which did well. Soon, everyone in Jamestown was growing good, sweet, tobacco leaf where once there had only been the rank leaf grown and smoked by the Indians. Large estates spread along the James River and the English dropped any attempt to fortify their homes.They had been at peace with the Indians for years and believed that all was well. Then Powhatan died and his successor decided to try to wipe out Jamestown.

## Massacre of the settlers

On March 22nd 1622, the Algonquin turned on the Jamestown colonists and murdered 347, men, women and children. Luckily for some of them a friendly Indian had warned them of the oncoming attack. If it had not been for this the whole colony could have been wiped out. The colonists were so friendly with the Indians that they were not prepared for any attack that may have come their way, so when the Algonquins did attack the English, they did not have any weapons prepared.

When the news of the attack reached London four months later, John Smith offered to take 130 soldiers out to Jamestown. He promised to 'torment the savages' and provide the colonists with arms. Sadly the Company turned his offer down claiming that they could not afford the expense and suggesting that Smith fund it himself. He stayed in London!

*( Kieron S.)*

Instead, the Company sent supplies of gunpowder to Virginia and King James sent a large shipment of arms from the Royal Armoury, much of which was obsolete, an early example of government surplus disposal.

Smith's next venture into print was a much more ambitious work, nothing less than a full-scale general history of the Virginia colony from the founding of Raleigh's colony at Roanoke in 1584 to 'today'. He started in 1621 and tried to persuade the Virginia Company to back the project. As usual, their problem and his was lack of money. By 1622, he had only completed 16 pages. In 1623, he issued a four page 'flyer' advertising the work, which had by then expanded to *'The general history of Virginia, New-England and the Summer Isles from their first beginnings'*. This brought him the rich backer he needed in the person of the 'Double Duchess', of Richmond and Lennox, Frances Howard. She had actually married three times, acquiring a considerable fortune. When her third husband died, she was probably one of the richest women in England.

Smith's history could now be completed and was published in July 1624.

Frances Howard, Duchess of Richmond and Lennox, *(from, the window in Willoughby Church)*

The magnificent cover of Smith's General History of 1624, showing all three monarchs, Elizabeth I, James I and Charles I, as Prince of Wales, a year before he came to the throne.

## 'History' or boasting ?

John Smith published his 'General History' at a time when there was a fashion for such works. Sir Walter Raleigh had used his time languishing as James's prisoner in the Tower of London to compile a 'History of the World' but he only completed the first section, from the Creation to 130 B.C. There are many 17th Century 'histories' still in existence. The one in the school library of King Edward VI Grammar School, Louth, is typical. It is a chronology, a series of tables of dates and events, from the beginning of the world, including the creation of Adam and Eve.

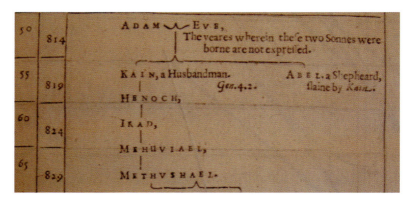

The record continues and lists all that happened right up to the 17th Century, with the founding of the Jamestown, recorded as 'Virginia planted', although the date is wrong!

John Smith's 'History' was very different. He took work from the writings of numerous other authors and combined these with his own writings to produce a work of six 'books'. The History covers Virginia, New England and the 'Summer Isles', now known as Bermuda.

For Smith, history was 'the memory of time, the life of the dead and the happiness of the living'. His own records of the story of Jamestown and New England were written in the third person and focused on 'what John Smith did', laying him open to a charge of boasting about his own achievements, but his book remains the most complete contemporary account of the founding and development of the English speaking colonies in Virginia, New England and Bermuda.

## The end of the Virginia Company

Just before John Smith's history was published, the Virginia Company was in real trouble. They had repeatedly raised money in London to send more settlers and supplies to Jamestown. Of those who had gone in 1607, just three remained alive. Of the thousands of young English, men and women who were tempted by promises of wealth and a new future, only 1200 survived. The Company's vain attempt to maintain 'good news from Virginia' had been a spectacular failure as disaster followed disaster. The only real success had been the development of tobacco growing but that put money into the pockets of the growers, not the Company share-holders. Jamestown changed from a military base to a plantation community. Eventually, it became a slave-owning society with a culture very different from that of New England, an unhappy image of the South which eventually led to the American Civil War.

But in 1623, King James appointed a commission to look into the Company's affairs and called for evidence. John Smith submitted his views. He was scathing of those who had sought to make a profit out of every aspect of the Colony's life, from overcharging for transporting men and supplies to sending out bond servants only to sell them on to Virginia settlers at a considerable mark-up. He criticised the Company's provision of many servants for each of the leaders, from the Governor downwards. Men who could have been given their own land to work for their own future prosperity were kept in indentured service and given no incentive to work hard.

In Smith's view the colony was in such a mess that the only solution was for the King to take over full control, which is precisely what happened. The Virginia Company was declared insolvent and the English settlement on the Chesapeake became the Royal Colony of Virginia, administered by a Governor appointed by the King.

Within a year, James I died and Charles I came to the throne. Another terrible outbreak of the plague killed 30,000 Londoners. It was not a good time to sell books on Virginia and Smith must have been relieved that the Double Duchess had paid his printing bill.

## Writing for seamen

Although John Smith never again set sail for America, he spent the last six years of his life writing and promoting the cause of new colonies in America. When war with Spain broke out again in 1626, England had to raise a new navy, having allowed the ships with which Drake and Raleigh defeated the Armada to rot away. Smith saw an opportunity to provide books which would both encourage young men to go to sea and to give them practical advice about manning ships

His first naval manual is a list of essential nautical terms which he called '*An accidence of the pathway to expeerience. Necessary for all young seamen, or those that are desirous to go to sea*'. Included is advice about nautical terms, on the duties of sailors and what to take on sea voyages, including *'the juyce of lemons for the scurvy'*. At least, something had been learnt from earlier suffering when many men had died for want of such good advice at the start of the Virginia voyages.

He also included a spirited account of what to do in a fight at sea…..

*'beare up close with him, with all your great and small shot charge him; board him on his weather quarter, lash fast you graplins and shear off, then run stemlins amid ships. Board and board or twart the hawse; we are foule on each other: the ship's on fire; cut anything to get clear and smother the fire with wet clothes; we are clear, and the fire is out, God be thanked.'*

The second was *'A Sea Grammar, with the Plaine Exposition of Smiths Accidence for young Sea-men'*, which Smith introduced with the comment : *'much hath bin written concerning the art of war by land, yet nothing concerning the same at sea'*. Much of the contents was taken from a manuscipt written by another nautical expert to which Smith added explanations of the terms which a young seaman had to know. These two books are the only two Smith wrote which were not directly linked to his own exploration of America, but they clearly come out of his wealth of experience of sailing and fighting at sea.

Next was the story of his life,

*'The True Travels, Adventures and Observations of Captaine John Smith, in Europe, Asia, Africa, and America from Anno Domini 1593 to 1629'.*

This extraordinary book was one of the first autobiographies ever printed. Many of Smith's early adventures are so unlikely that many have accused him of lying, but most recent studies have suggested that the details of what he wrote are probably true. At least no-one can prove that he was lying!

What comes across throughout this book is his unshakeable self-confidence and conviction that by his own efforts he could rise from a relatively lowly background to the leadership of men. Although he was helped by the Willoughby family, those others who considered themselves his social superiors consistently got in his way – not that this stopped him!

## Promoting a new model for colonies

Finally, Smith wrote his most important book,

*'Advertisments for the Unexperienced Planters of New England, or Anywhere. Or, the Path-way to Experience to Erect a Plantation'*

Published in London in 1631, it was written at a time when, in the poet George Herbert's words,

> *'Religion stands on tiptoe in our land,*
> *Ready to pass to the American strand.'*

Charles I had inherited his father's deep objection to those who wished to reform the Church of England from within, the Puritans, and to those who wanted to break free altogether, the Separatists. He also shared his father's conviction that God had given him the right to be king and that it was therefore his subjects' role to obey his commands and support his proposals.

This approach to social status, from the King downwards, was still thought proper three hundred years later as the Victorian children's hymn made all too clear:

*The rich man in his castle*
*The poor man at his gate,*
*He made them high and lowly*
*And ordered their estate.*

*All things bright and beautiful....*

Charles I by Abigail M.

Charles particularly disliked the Puritans in the Church and many of their leaders were increasingly interested in leaving England to find a new future in America. William Laud, who was to be appointed by Charles as Archbishop of Canterbury, believed that services in church should all follow the pattern set out in the Book of Common Prayer, which many Puritans found deeply objectionable. Just as James I had declared that he would make the clergy of the Church of England conform to the authorised practices of the church, or 'harry them out of the land', so Laud and his fellow

Bishops demanded that all the clergy comply with the services and practices which were required by the church authorities.

Some, like the Vicar of Boston, John Cotton, realised that they could no longer minister in the Church of England and must go elsewhere, just as the leaders of the Pilgrim Fathers had done about twenty years before.

Archbishop William Laud by Alice S.

Members of John Cotton's congregation in Boston, Lincolnshire, linked up with John Winthrop of Suffolk and the family of the Earl of Lincoln at Tattershall to plan a new colony. They read John Smith's books on New England and studied his map. When they got to New England and recorded their experience, the author of one account actually advised those who wanted to follow them to buy Smith's books and use them well.

At the end of his 'True Travels', published in 1630, Smith wrote about the 'company of people of good rank, zeal, means and quality who first sailed to New England in 1629'. After this first party, who settled at Salem,

Massachusetts, the main group of over five hundred colonists sailed with John Winthrop in 1630. The farewell sermon which John Cotton preached to those on the Arbella is commemorated in the window in Boston Parish Church.

John Cotton preaching a sermon to the Massachusetts Bay settlers before they left on the Arbella

This was the group that founded Boston, Massachusetts and started the 'great migration' to New England.

## Father of New England?

The Englishman who has been called 'the Father of New England' is William Brewster, who in 1608 led the Scrooby Separatists on a long journey out of England, to Holland and then, as the Pilgrim Fathers, to Plymouth Plantation in America.

John Smith could claim the same title as he regarded all the early English settlements as his children, or as a former farmer put it 'pigs of my sow'. In that part of his

'General History' covering New England, Smith wrote of the first American colonies:

*'I may call them my children; for they have been my wife, my hawks, my hounds, my cards, my dice and in total my best contentas indifferent to my heart, as my left hand to my right. And not withstanding all those miracles of disaster have crossed both them and me, yet were there not an Englishman remaining, as God be thanked notwithstanding the massacre there are some thousands; I would begin again with as small means as I did at first…..*

## 'The most admired people'

Smith received little reward for his achievements. In an age when knighthoods and baronetcies were 'sold' by a King short of funds, he remained plain 'Captain John'. He never returned to live in his native Lincolnshire, preferring to remain in or near London as the guest of one or another of his wealthy friends. Many of these were members of prominent Puritan families, such as the Mildmays and the Saltonstalls.

Smith fitted well into their households, as one who was never known to smoke tobacco, drink strong liquor or swear, but he was not much interested in theology, remaining a loyal member of the 'King's Church', or as he put it 'a good Catholic Protestant according to the reformed Church of England'. He dedicated one of his books to both the High Church Archbishop of York and the Puritan Archbishop of Canterbury of the time, ensuring that neither faction could claim him as a supporter.

His vision of America was of a land of opportunity, where a man 'may be master and owner of his own labour and land', where *'if he have nothing but his hands, he may set up his trade and by industry quickly grow rich'*. With so much land available, men coming to New England who were 'good honest labourers' should be given as much land and freedom as possible. *'Therefore let all men have as much freedom in reason as may be true dealing, for it is the greatest comfort you can give them.'* Smith had bitter memories of the *'thousand Gallants as were sent to me, that would do nothing but complain, curse and despair, when they saw our miseries and all things so clean contrary to the report in England'*.

Frustrated in Virginia by the attempt of the London Company to manage the Colony from the other side of the Atlantic, Smith saw the huge benefits of a colony managing its own affairs. *'They can make no laws in Virginia, till they be ratified in England'*, he wrote bitterly, and he applauded the decision of the leaders of the Massachusetts Bay Colony to take their Charter with them. This enabled them to set up a self-governing community, albeit still under the authority of the English Crown. It would take another 150 years for the people of America to challenge that authority and win their freedom from the British.

Finally, at the end of his *'Advertisements'*, his last published work, he wrote:

*'Lastly remember as faction, pride and security (over-confidence), produces nothing but confusion, misery and dissolution; so the contraries well practised will in short time make you happy, and the most admired people of all our plantations for your time in the world'*.

## John Smith's Death

After years of people trying to kill him, the Spanish, the Turks, the Virginian Indians, the French and even some of the English, John Smith died in bed of natural causes.

Right up to his death, he carried on writing and promoting the colonisation of America. By the summer of 1631, just a few months after he finished his last book, he was probably in the house of his long term friend, Sir Samuel Saltonstall. On June 21st, Smith died at the age of fifty one, the end of a long and adventurous life. He made his mark on his last will and testament, putting aside twenty pounds from his estate to pay for his own funeral. There was enough to buy wine for his mourners as they gathered to laugh and maybe cry and speak of his adventures and mishaps. Then Smith's remains were carried inside St Sepulchre's Church, Newgate, London, where he was laid to rest. On the wall above his tomb, a tablet was hung:

> *'Here lies one conquer'd that hath conquered Kings'*
> *Subdu'd large territories, and done things*
> *Which to the world imposible would seem*
> *But that the truth is held in more esteeme.'*

Thirty five years later, the church was burnt down in the Great Fire of 1666. The exact spot of his grave was lost and the tablet over Smith's grave was destroyed. Of all the Englishmen who were involved in the settlement of North America, John Smith made the greatest contribution to the new nation in which the 'American Dream' was born. Or as one 21st century student put it:

*John Smith*    *(Sean P.)*

*It was at the house of Saltonstall,*
*Where John Smith died;*
*Englishmen hardly know him at all,*
*For going to America battling the tide.*

*Gunpowder was on his lap,*
*While he took a nap.*
*A spark; he was burnt waist to knee,*
*Then dived into the sea.*

*A boat to England he took  
And published his book,  
From the parcel of his notes  
About his days on the boats.*

*In the Atlantic Ocean  
The pirate ship fired a gun  
They took his boat by storm,  
John Smith was left forlorn.*

*Onto the sand  
At last, dry land.  
He had no kids or even a wife,  
Instead he had an exciting life.*

*Then he travelled home at last,  
But that is gone, it's in the past,  
Survived 51 years of enemy rage  
But died of certain death, old age!*

Smith wrote his own sad epitaph, and so he should have the last word, as he always wanted!

> The Sea Marke.

*'Aloofe, aloofe, and come no neare,  
   the dangers doe appeare;  
Which if my ruine had not beene  
    you had not seene  
  I onely lie upon this shelfe  
    To be a marke to all  
which on the same might fall,  
That none may perish but my selfe.*

(From the introduction of his last work 'Advertisements for the Unxperienced' 1631)

# Postscript

If you want to know the true story of what happened to Pocahontas, the Indian Princess who twice saved John Smith's life, read the next book in the ARIES series 'Mrs John Rolfe, better known as Pocahontas'. Thirteen years after Jamestown was first established, the Pilgrim Fathers landed at Plymouth near Cape Cod and established their settlement. Ten years after that, the Massachusetts Bay Company founded the large colony which grew into the City of Boston, Massachusetts. Not long after the city of Boston, Massachusetts was founded, the Catholics established their first settlements in Maryland. All these developments in early American history have their roots in the rich soil of Eastern England, but the first was Jamestown. In 2007, the 400th anniversary of the founding of America will be celebrated in Virginia and in England.

## Captain John Smith – outline chronology

| | |
|---|---|
| 1492 | Columbus 'discovers' the New World |
| 1509 | Henry VIII becomes king |
| 1536 | Lincolnshire Rising |
| 1547 | Edward VI becomes king |
| 1553 | Mary becomes queen |
| 1558 | Elizabeth I becomes Queen |
| 1564 | William Shakespeare born |
| 1580 | John Smith baptized on 9th January |
| 1588 | Defeat of the Spanish Armada |
| 1590 | Shakespeare's first plays, 1 and 2 Henry VI, performed |
| 1595? | Pocahontas born; Smith works for merchant in Lynn |
| 1596 | Worst harvest of the century; Smith's father dies |
| 1599 | Globe Theatre opens in Southwark |

| | |
|---|---|
| 1600? | Smith goes off to fight the Turks |
| 1603 | James VI of Scotland succeeds Elizabeth as James I of England; plague in London |
| 1604 | Smith is back in London; Hampton Court Conference; peace with Spain |
| 1605 | Gunpowder Plot fails |
| 1606 | First Virginia Company Charter December, three ships sail for Virginia |
| 1607 | Ships arrive in Virginia; Jamestown settled |
| 1608 | Smith elected President for one year |
| 1609 | Smith injured and has to return to England |
| 1610 | Smith starts to write his 2nd book on Virginia Galileo observes moons of Jupiter |
| 1611 | 'King James Bible' published; Shakespeare's last well-known play, The Tempest, first performed |
| 1612 | 2nd Virginia Company Charter; Smith's 'A Map of Virginia' published in Oxford |
| 1614 | Smith sails to 'northen Virginia' mapping the coast from Maine to Cape Cod |
| 1614 | Pocahontas marries John Rolfe |
| 1615 | Smith given title 'Admiral of New England' |
| 1615 | Smith sails again for New England but is captured by French pirates |
| 1616 | Smith's book 'A Description of New England' is published in London |
| 1616 | John Rolfe and Pocahontas visit London |
| 1617 | Pocahontas dies at Gravesend |
| 1618 | Sir Walter Raleigh executed |
| 1620 | Pilgrim Fathers settle at Plymouth, Massachusetts; Smith's 'New England Trials' published |
| 1623 | Dutch settle New Amsterdam which later becomes New York |

| | |
|---|---|
| 1624 | Smith's 'The General History of Virginia, New-England and the Summer Isles' published in London |
| 1625 | Charles I becomes king; plague in London |
| 1626/7 | Smith's two books on seafaring published |
| 1630 | Massachusetts Bay company establishes new settlement at Boston, Massachusetts |
| 1631 | John Smith dies in London |
| 1634 | Catholic settlers establish colony of Maryland |
| 1649 | Charles I executed |

## Sources

We used the following sources to research this book

Arber, Edward Ed.
    'Travels and Works of Captain John Smith ' 2nd Ed.
    A.G Bradley Edinburgh 1910
Barbour, Philip
    'Pocahontas and her World' Robert Hale 1969
    'The Three Worlds of Captain John Smith'.
    Houghton
    Miflin. 1964
Doherty, Kieron
    'To Conquer is to Live' Twenty-first Century 2001 *
Hume, Ivor Noel
    'The Virginia Adventure'. Knopf. 1994
Kelso, William and Beverley Straube
    'Jamestown Rediscovery 1994-2004' APVA 2004
Kupperman, Karen Ordahl
    'Captain John Smith – a selection of his writings'
    Univ of North Carolina Press 1988
Lemay, J A Leo
    'The American Dream of Captain John Smith' UPV.
    1991

Mello, Tara Baukus
    *'John Smith'* Chelsea House 2000*
Parker, Michael St John
    *'William Shakespeare'*. Pitkin.2000
Price, David A
    *'Love and Hate in Jamestown'* Knopf. 2003
Shakespeare, William
    *Complete Works* Ed. Peter Alexander. Collins. 1951
Smith, Bradford
    *'Captain John Smith'* Lipincott. 1953
Wright Hale, Edward
    *'Jamestown Narratives'*. Roundhouse. 1998
Zucker Stanley, Melanie
    *'John Smith'* Foxhound 2000*

* books written for young people

# Thanks

Many individuals have helped us to write and illustrate this book and we would like to thank them all:

James Wheeldon, Headmaster, and the Governors of King Edward VI Grammar School, Louth; Richard Gurnham, Aimie Reeves, Helen Appleton, Toni Folen, Shakila Roy, Julie Roberts and Carole Ashcroft of King Edward VI Grammar School, Louth;  Molly Burkett of Barny Books, Geof Allinson of Allinson Print and Supplies; Philip Peck, Jenny Haden

and many others who have helped with layout advice, historical information and patience when our interest in American history got in the way of other priorities.